¡MARIMBA!

Animales from A to Z

by Pat Mora

Illustrated by Doug Cushman

CLARION BOOKS

New York

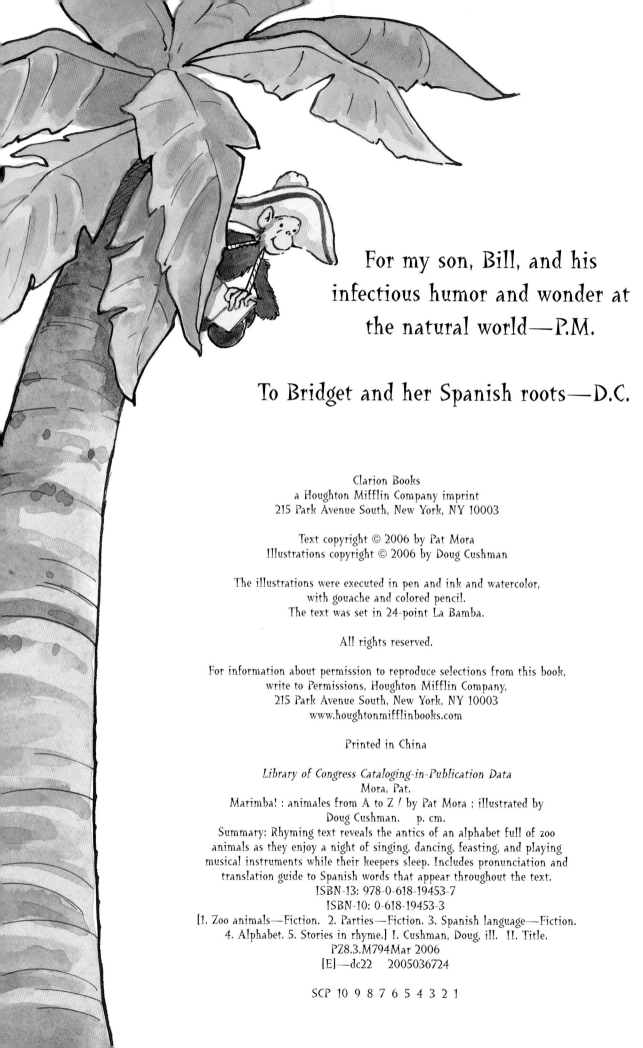

For my son, Bill, and his
infectious humor and wonder at
the natural world—P.M.

To Bridget and her Spanish roots—D.C.

Clarion Books
a Houghton Mifflin Company imprint
215 Park Avenue South, New York, NY 10003

Text copyright © 2006 by Pat Mora
Illustrations copyright © 2006 by Doug Cushman

The illustrations were executed in pen and ink and watercolor,
with gouache and colored pencil.
The text was set in 24-point La Bamba.

Printed in China

Library of Congress Cataloging-in-Publication Data
Mora, Pat.
Marimba! : animales from A to Z / by Pat Mora ; illustrated by
Doug Cushman.   p. cm.
Summary: Rhyming text reveals the antics of an alphabet full of zoo
animals as they enjoy a night of singing, dancing, feasting, and playing
musical instruments while their keepers sleep. Includes pronunciation and
translation guide to Spanish words that appear throughout the text.
ISBN-13: 978-0-618-19453-7
ISBN-10: 0-618-19453-3
[1. Zoo animals—Fiction. 2. Parties—Fiction. 3. Spanish language—Fiction.
4. Alphabet. 5. Stories in rhyme.] I. Cushman, Doug, ill. II. Title.
PZ8.3.M794Mar 2006
[E]—dc22   2005036724

SCP 10 9 8 7 6 5 4 3 2 1

Once a year, the singing monkey croons the keepers to sleep at the zoo.

Then the ting-tong of the marimba
wakes all *animales* on cue.

Bobcats and bears dance *la bamba*.
Burros bray, "Bravo! Repeat!"

6

"Let's conga," say cougars to *coyotes*,
"to marimba's ting-tong beat!"

D

Seals and frisky *delfines*
leap over cacti and trees.

E

They startle the *elefantes*
who ting-tong tango with chimpanzees.

When *flamencos* practice flamenco,
frogs and fish shimmy and prance.

Gorilas strum their guitars,
and gophers country dance.

11

Hipopótamos practice the hula,
in a happy hullabaloo.

Iguanas practice the cha-cha
to marimba's ting-tong at the zoo.

Juncos chirp to *jaguares*,
"Please taste this delicious flan."

K

Koalas serve enchiladas
to a hungry orangutan.

A chorus of lions and *llamas*
samba down the street.

Mariachi *manatees* mambo
to marimba's ting-tong beat.

 Nanny goats and *nutrias*
gobble salads of nuts and flowers.

Otters and *ocelotes*
make piñatas for hours and hours.

Pandas juggle papayas
in the peccaries' parade.

Scurrying quail and *quetzales*
sell ice-cold lemonade.

R

Raccoons and *rinocerontes*
rumba with rattlesnakes.

Sloths and *salamandras*
salsa around the lakes.

¡Ay no!

Tigers hear *tucanes*
Clack warnings with noisy beaks.

U

Wearing horns like *unicornios*,
horses loudly neigh, *"Eeeeek! Eeeeek!"*

Vultures tell *vicuñas,*
"The keepers are all awake!"

W

Woodpeckers warn *wapities,*
"¡*Pronto!* Finish your chocolate cake!"

27

X

Parrots cover *xilófonos*
and the calliope.

Yellowbirds and wacky *yakes*
hide in the shrubbery.

But then,

Z

zigzagging through zebras and *zebúes*,
zany keepers call, "Yoo-hooooooooooooo,"

and join the singing and dancing
to marimba's ting-tong at the zoo.

AUTHOR'S NOTE

After writing the counting book *Uno, Dos, Tres/One, Two, Three*, I wanted to create an alphabet book that incorporated both English and Spanish. I looked for twenty-six cognates—words similar in both languages—so that Spanish speakers would discover they are already familiar with twenty-six words in English, and English speakers would find they already know some Spanish.

Languages, rich and complex human creations, steadily borrow words from other languages. Cognates share origins or root words and often share meanings. Romance languages that flow from Latin, for example, change *nox*, the word for night, into *notte* (Italian), *noite* (Portuguese), *nuit* (French), and *noche* (Spanish).

Like Latin American cultures themselves, this book has rhythm and movement. The mischievous monkey plays a marimba, a wood instrument much like a xylophone, and the animals dance the bamba, conga, flamenco, cha-cha, samba, rumba, salsa, and tango. Although origins of the tango are associated with Argentina, and salsa with Cuba, most Latin American dances have complex roots and a rich combination of Latin, Afro-Caribbean, and European origins. Foods mentioned in the book—enchiladas (corn tortillas served rolled or flat with chicken, beef, shrimp, or cheese, and covered with chili sauce) and flan (creamy caramel custard)—also have complex origins.

Enjoy the fiesta!

TRANSLATION & PRONUNCIATION GUIDE

animales (ah-nee-MAH-lehs): animals

burros
(BOO-rohs):
donkeys

coyotes
(coh-YOH-tehs):
coyotes

delfínes
(del-FEE-nehs):
dolphins

elefantes
(el-eh-FAHN-tehs):
elephants

flamencos
(fla-MEHN-cohs)
flamingos

gorilas
(goh-REE-lahs):
gorillas

hipopótamos
(hee-poh-POH-tah mohs):
hippopotamuses

iguanas
(ee-GWAH-nahs):
iguanas

jaguares
(ha-GWAH-rehs):
jaguars

koalas
(ko-AH-lahs):
koalas

llamas
(YAH-mahs):
llamas

manatíes
(mah-nah-TEE-ehs): manatees

nutrias
(NOO-tree-ahs):
nutrias

ocelotes
(oh-seh-LOH-tehs):
ocelots

pandas
(PAHN-dahs):
pandas

quetzales
(keht-SAH-lehs):
quetzals

rinocerontes
(ree-noh-se-ROHN-tehs): rhinoceros

salamandras
(sah-lah-MAHN-drahs):
salamanders

tucánes
(too-CAH-nehs):
toucans

unicornios
(oo-nee-COHR-nyohs): unicorns

vicuñas
(vee-KOO-nyahs):
vicuñas

wapitíes
(wah-pee-TEE-ehs):
wapitis

xilófonos
(see-LOH-foh-nohs):
xylophones

yakes
(YAH-kehs):
yaks

zebúes*
(seh-BOO-ehs):
zebus
*sometimes spelled
cebúes